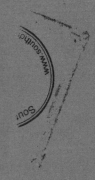

Words
and your
heart

Kate Jane Neal

SIMON & SCHUSTER
London   New York   Sydney   Toronto   New Delhi

For Thea, Toby, Isaac and Summer x

SIMON & SCHUSTER
First published in Great Britain in 2017 by Simon & Schuster UK Ltd,
1st Floor, 222 Gray's Inn Road, London WC1X 8HB • A CBS Company
This edition published in 2018 • Text and illustrations copyright ©
2017 Kate Jane Neal • The right of Kate Jane Neal to be identified as
the author and illustrator of this work has been asserted by her in
accordance with the Copyright, Designs and Patents Act, 1988 • All
rights reserved, including the right of reproduction in whole or in part
in any form • A CIP catalogue record for this book is available from the
British Library upon request • Printed in China
ISBN: 978-1-4711-6856-7 (HB)
ISBN: 978-1-4711-6853-6 (PB)
ISBN: 978-1-4711-6854-3 (eBook) • 10 9 8 7 6 5 4 3 2 1

This book is about your heart.

The little bit inside of you that makes you, you!

Will you listen *really* carefully?

Because it's **REALLY** . . .

IMPORTANT!

And it might help you
be a happier you,

and the people around you,
be a happier them!

You see, the **WORDS** that go into your ears . . .

. . . can actually affect your heart!

The little bit inside of you that makes you, you!

Your  can do . . .

AMAZING
things!

They can
describe
things if
they are

BIG ...

Or if they are *little*.

They can explain stuff, so you know that it goes . . .

Whizz,
whoosh,
BOOM!

Or spin, tinkle, **PING**!

Words can make you happy . . .

. . . and make you want to sing!

Larrrrrrrrrr

But sometimes words can make us cry.

We all know what sort of words they are.

You see, sometimes words can be like a deadly arrow,
that can pierce someone's heart.

The little bit inside of them that makes them, them!

And some words can really hurt.

Your WORDS have POWER

DUN DUN DARrr

Your words can actually change
the way someone's heart feels.

The little bit inside of them that makes them, them!

If someone feels sad . . .

. . . your words can cheer them up!

If someone feels weak,
your words can help them feel stronger.

If someone wants to give up . . .

. . . your words can help keep them going.

Make them giggle,

make them grin,

make them laugh out loud and roll around!

Do you see what we mean?

Your **words** are

amazing

and

POWERFUL

How about we all use our
words to look after each
other's hearts?

*The little bit inside of us that makes us, **us**!*

Let's try together and see the difference it makes.

Today, somebody's world can be
a better place, because of you!

Doesn't that make your

heart

feel

good!